J.A. Udden

Fossil Ice Crystals

Outlook

J.A. Udden

Fossil Ice Crystals

1. Auflage | ISBN: 978-3-73262-107-1

Erscheinungsort: Frankfurt am Main, Deutschland

Erscheinungsjahr: 2018

Outlook Verlag GmbH, Frankfurt.

Reproduction of the original.

Fossil Ice Crystals
An Instance of the Practical Value of "Pure Science"

Bureau of Economic Geology and Technology
Division of Economic Geology
J. A. Udden, Director of the Bureau and Head of the Division

Published by the University six times a month and entered as second-class matter at the postoffice at
AUSTIN, TEXAS

The benefits of education and of useful knowledge, generally diffused through a community, are essential to the preservation of a free government.

Sam Houston

Cultivated mind is the guardian genius of democracy.... It is the only dictator that freemen acknowledge and the only security that freemen desire.

Mirabeau B. Lamar

FOSSIL ICE CRYSTALS

By J. A. Udden

AN INSTANCE OF THE PRACTICAL VALUE OF "PURE SCIENCE"

The practical value of the service of the geological profession is, with every year, being more and more appreciated, especially among people who are developing the mineral resources of our country. Nevertheless, we still hear men who speak of geologists as theorists that render our profitable industries but little assistance. It is true that much of the work that geologists do has but a remote bearing on practical questions. The fact is that in geology, as in other sciences, one can never know when a purely scientific observation may turn out to have a practical application. Paleontologists who study the minutest details of fossils have been held up as impractical people, even though their science has more than once proved to be of the greatest practical importance for the finding of valuable natural deposits. Certainly those who have been most prominent in the promotion of paleontology as a science have seldom, if ever, had any economic motive in the pursuit of their work. I think the same is true of our leading petrographers. I believe that the men who have advanced the science of geology most, have seldom contributed much to the practical application of the principles they have discovered. Much scientific work naturally appears unprofitable or useless to the uninitiated. I shall here relate a case that suggests how entirely wrong it may be to regard as of no economic value any geologic fact, however insignificant it may appear.

In the summer of 1890 I took occasion to make a trip to the Black Hills in South Dakota in order to profit, as I could, by a few weeks' tramping in this interesting region. Going one day in a southwest direction from Minnekahta, to look for fossil cycads, I stumbled on a block of sandstone with a rather smooth surface on which were some peculiar markings, such as I had never seen figured or described. The rock was evidently a block from the Dakota sandstone. Its smooth upper surface, which represented a bedding plane, was covered with a thin coating of silt or fine clay which adhered to the block. The markings were in this clay. They were straight, shallow grooves from one-half to two inches in length, and from one-sixteenth to one-eighth inch in width. They were joined into patterns in which some sprang out from the sides of others and again themselves sent out other branches. Some crossed each other. I noticed that there was a quite uniform angle of divergence in these branches, and I was able to make out that this usual angle was about sixty degrees. I also noted that the grooves narrowed to sharp points. Somehow, immediately I concluded that the cracks were the result of ice crystals, and I at once saw the propriety of frozen water having existed in an age during which deciduous trees began to appear. This was theory. We have since that time learned to know that cold climates far antedate the coming of the dicotyledons.

As I had no suitable photographic equipment, I took pains to make accurate drawings of a part of the pattern as it appeared on the rock. My original drawing is shown in Plate I. A brief description of these markings was later furnished in the Scientific American, of February 19, 1895.

It took me some years to find any similar markings again. In the early spring of 1903 I had occasion to make a visit to Mexico, when I spent a half day in Ojinaga, which is a little village south of Presidio, in Texas, on the Mexican side of the river. Some sidewalks in this little village are built of flags of limestone belonging to the Eagle Ford formation. To my great delight I found some of these slabs having precisely the same kind of markings that I had noted on the sandstone in Dakota. Naturally I attached some importance to the fact that the Eagle Ford corresponds quite closely in age to that of the Dakota sandstone. Both were made at about the beginning of the upper Cretaceous age. I noticed here a considerable variation in the closeness of the patterns of the markings. Occasionally they were found as separate single lines, several inches removed from each other; and on other rocks they would be found crossing in close networks. In the summer of 1904 I again found my ice markings on a layer of arenaceous limestone in the same formation in the Big Bend country in Texas. This time I collected some specimens which were subsequently photographed. One of these photographs is shown in Plate II. Again in 1906 I noticed the same markings on some thin sandy flags which occur in the Del Rio clay near the city of Del Rio. In this case the needle-like crystals were somewhat more slender than those previously seen, and some were slightly curved and somewhat more elongated. These of course interested me as showing the occurrence of freezing temperatures no doubt at a somewhat earlier time than that pertaining to my previous observations.

During all these years my residence was in Illinois, and I was naturally watching for similar markings in recent mud, resulting from late and early frosts. I found them in the fall of 1909. At this time some excavations were being made in the loess in Rock Island, when some rains fell in the late fall. These rains evidently happened to give the mud the amount of moisture necessary for such crystals to develop, as the ground froze. The rains had washed the loess extensively, and I found a number of places where it lay redistributed, with a fairly smooth surface. It was evident that the moisture content of the ground, together with the temperature conditions, determined the size and the closeness of the frozen patterns. In places the crystals were long and slender, in others they were short and stout. At some points they were straight and in others slightly curved. Here and there the patterns were close enough to resemble the fine lines which we sometimes notice in the hoarfrost on windowpanes. In other places the crystals occurred in radiating groups, and elsewhere they would form scattered separate units. For preserving a record of what I saw, I poured plaster over several patterns and had these casts photographed, as appears in Plates VIII, IX, X. Placing these side by side with the photographs of the patterns I have photographed from the Eagle Ford, it appears to me that no doubt can be left as to the origin of the markings found in the fossil state.

Recently I have found that these ice crystal marks are quite common at one horizon in the Eagle Ford beds of Brewster County, in Texas. There is also a layer in which they can be usually seen in the vicinity of Austin, Texas. This lies about twenty-five feet below the Austin Chalk, near Austin. A like layer occurs about 100 feet below the Austin Chalk in the Big Bend country. Here I have found the markings in localities thirty miles apart. They occur at the north point of Mariscal Mountain and in a number of places near the Fossil Knobs and on the Chisos Mining Company property at Terlingua.

Unprofitable as observations on such a simple matter as this may seem, I find that other geologists have given it some attention. Quite recently, Dr. John M. Clarke[A] has figured slabs showing what has been described as *Fucoides graphica*, by Hall. The markings figured by Professor Clarke are undoubtedly of the same kind as those I have found in the Eagle Ford. They occur in the Upper Devonian in New York. I also find that the formation of ice crystals in wet mud has been observed in the clays about Boston by Marbut and Woodworth.[B] Other observations of similar recent markings are said to have been made by some English geologists.

To "practical people" it may indeed appear that no more unprofitable or more idle curiosity could be indulged in, than making observations on what kind of crystals are formed when water freezes in mud. I must confess that my own first observations had no motive whatever, except for the desire to know something new; and I never expected that anything I could learn about these fossil marks would ever turn out to have any practical application, at least not in my own work.

But it has turned out differently. For some time, I have been called upon occasionally to advise with regard to the finding of the ore in one of our quicksilver mines in West Texas. It is now a well established fact that the distribution of the ore in this mine, and I believe in the entire Terlingua district, bears a definite relation to geological horizons. Successful mining requires search in these horizons. The cinnabar, as it appears, has accumulated in greatest quantity under impervious rocks such as shales and marls along planes that separate these from underlying rocks of more open texture, mostly limestones. The ore has clearly come from below and has risen through fissure planes, which in some cases separate large blocks of the Cretaceous formations. The best ore has been found under the basal part of the Boquillas flags, and under the Del Rio clay in the upper part of the Georgetown limestone. The workings must be so arranged in the mine that these horizons can be entered on both sides of a fault fissure. The problem of locating the depth of the desirable horizons in the mine in question would be easy enough, if it were not for the fact that the outcropping rocks consist of a series of sediments with few characteristic fossils. Most of the fossils which occur extend through a range of several hundred feet and the beds themselves are quite uniform in character, consisting of alternating thin layers of impure limestones and marls. An attempt was made to correlate the outcropping beds by close examination of the layers exposed, but the result was not very satisfactory. A close scrutiny made of each layer on the section resulted, however, in the finding of two features that enabled me to measure the throw of the fault under investigation. Interbedded in the Boquillas flags there are some thin layers of bentonite, which are quite persistent and can be followed for several miles. By comparing the distances between these layers and by taking note of their individual thickness, it was possible to make a correlation that seemed to be correct. But the proof sought fell just short of being certain. In cases of this kind one always looks for corroborating facts to check one's conclusions. I found this check in the discovery of the layer which carries ice crystal markings in these beds. The layer had a definite relation to the seams of bentonite, and, with this additional evidence, I was confident there was no possible chance of a mistake. It enabled me to locate not only the right horizon but also a horizon in the underlying heavy Comanchean limestone, which is water-bearing, and which must be avoided to prevent serious injury to the underground operations. I need not add that the information obtained was of real practical value in this case.

PLATE I

Plate I. Formsof frost cracks seen on the exposed flat bedding plane of a block of Dakota sandstone in a ravine a few miles southwest of Minnekahta, South Dakota. As ketched in the field. Natural size.

Plate I

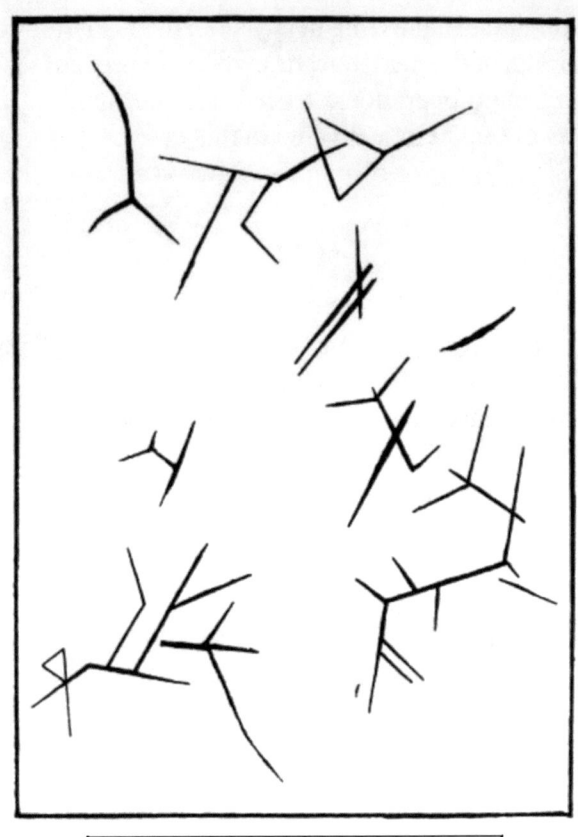

PLATE II

Plate II. Photographs of fossil imprints of ice crystals on flags of the Eagle Ford. The upper rock shown in the Plate is from the south side of Cuesta Blanca in Brewster County, Texas, and shows casts of crystals which represent fillings of sandy mud projecting slightly down into an underlying bed of more argillaceous material. The lower part of the figure shows a similarly marked flag from the same formation at a point about five miles north of the old Boquillas postoffice near Tornillo Creek, east of the Chisos

Mountains, in Texas. Here are seen the original grooves made by the ice on a layer of muddy material later buried. Slightlyreduced.

Plate II

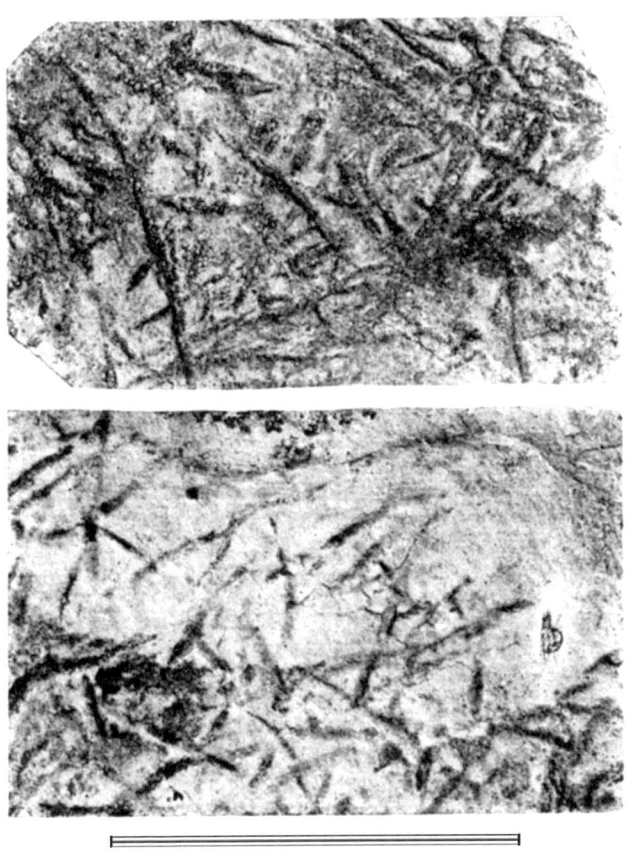

PLATE III

Plate III. Photographof fossil casts of a close tangle of ice crystals seen in a stony calcareous layer in the Eagle Ford shale in Walnut Creek, about eight miles north of Austin, Texas. This tangle is closer than any of the recent ice crystal marks figured here, but equally closely grown crystals have been seen by the writer on

frozen mud in Illinois. Naturalsize. Comparewith Plate VIII.
Plate III

PLATE IV

Plate IV. Photographof fossil casts of ice crystals seen on some stony flags in the upper part of the Eagle Ford at Fossil Knobs, about two miles northwest of the Chisos Mine in Brewster County, Texas. These may be characterized as relatively short and scattered. This shows ridges projecting into the grooves formed by ice crystals on the surface of a muddy layer originally underlying the

layer photographed. Slightlyreduced.
Plate IV

PLATE V

Plate V. Photograph of fossil casts of ice crystals seen on the under side of flaggy layer of calcareous sandy rock in the upper part of the Eagle Ford at Fossil Knobs, about two miles northwest from the Chisos Mining Company's property, Brewster County, Texas. It will be seen that some of the crystals are gently curved. Similar curving crystals are also seen in the figures showing recent growths

at Rock Island, Illinois.   Compare with Plate IX.   Slightly reduced.
Plate V

PLATE VI

Plate VI. Photograph of a thin flag of sandy limestone from the Eagle Ford at Fossil Knobs in Brewster County, showing molds left by ice crystals.

Plate VI

PLATE VII

Plate VII. Photographs of three fragments of flags showing casts of ice crystals on the under side. All observations made on crystals of this kind indicate local differences in the forms of ice crystals presumably due to differences in the rate of freezing, in the texture of the mud and probably in variations in water content of the mud. Some crystals in the locality from which these specimens came, show pinnate secondary growths. Specimens shown here are from near the upper part of the Eagle Ford at a point about two miles north from the Chisos Mining Company's property. Brewster County, Texas. Slightly reduced.

Plate VII

PLATE VIII

Plate VIII. Photograph of a cast made by pouring plaster over a surface of mud in which ice crystals had recently formed, in Rock Island, Illinois, after the ice in the crystals had been removed by slow natural sublimation into the atmosphere, leaving open cracks in the mud. The comb-like ridges on the plaster cast have the form

of the ice crystals. Compare with Plate III.
Plate VIII

PLATE IX

Plate IX. Photograph of a cast made by pouring plaster over a surface of mud in which ice crystals had formed, in Rock Island, Illinois, soon after the ice in the crystals had been removed by slow natural sublimation into the atmosphere, leaving open cracks in the mud. In the locality where this cast was made, the crystals were relatively slender, distant, and some gently curved, like those seen in Plate V. Slightlyreduced.

Plate IX

PLATE X

Plate X. Photographof a cast made by pouring plaster over a surface of mud in which ice crystals had recently formed, in Rock Island, Ill., and where they had later been removed by natural sublimations into the atmosphere, leaving open cracks in the mud. It will be seen that the crystal growth in this case involves an x-like or radiating pattern formed of relatively very slender forms that almost everywhere are very gently curved somewhat reminding of the slender thread-like crystals sometimes seen in frost on windows. I have not yet seen any similar fossil crystal growths as slender as these. Slightlyreduced.

Plate X

FOOTNOTES:

A Strand and undertow markings, etc., New York State Museum, *Bulletin No. 196, April 1, 1917*, pp. 199-210; pl. 20-23.

B Brick clays of Rhode Island, Massachusetts; Marbut and Woodworth, *U.S. Geol. Survey, 17th Ann. Rep., Pt. 1*, p. 992.